k   l

DIANE KELLY

Copyright © 2022 Diane Kelly

All Rights Reserved

No part of this book may be reproduced, downloaded, transmitted, decompiled, reverse engineered, stored in, or introduced to any information storage and retrieval system, in any form, whether electronic or mechanical, without the author's prior written permission. Scanning, uploading, or distribution of this book via the Internet or any other means without permission is prohibited. Federal law requires that consumers purchase only authorized electronic versions and provides for criminal and civil penalties for producing or possessing pirated copies.

This book is a work of fiction. Names, characters, organizations, places, events, and incidents are either used fictitiously or products of the author's imagination. Any resemblance to actual persons, living or dead, or actual events is entirely coincidental.

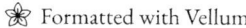 Formatted with Vellum

Chapter One

Sherlock lay in a sphinx pose in front of the only window in our small studio apartment, gazing down at the street three stories below. Though all cats are curious, my brown tabby was exceptionally so. He spent most of his time at the glass—between naps, of course—carefully watching the comings and goings of our neighbors and the many tourists who strolled by to admire the houses. Even though Savannah's historic Victorian District tended to be calm and peaceful, he took his duties quite seriously.

While Sherlock performed his surveillance, I sat at the small wooden table in our tiny converted attic space, cramming for an upcoming exam. I'm a Preservation Design major at Savannah College of Art and Design, SCAD for short. I love old houses, especially the Victorians like the one my cat and I currently lived in. It was probably a pipe dream, but I hoped to live in a sprawling Victorian of my own someday. But even if I'd never own one myself, I'd be spending lots of time in such houses once I graduated. My studies in Preservation Design would enable me to restore old buildings to their former glory. Ironically, the class I was studying for today was called "Modern Architecture Before 1900." *Could anything built before 1900 really be called modern?* I supposed it could have been so-called at the time.

At 1:45, the alarm on my cell phone went off, reminding me it was time to head next door. I closed my book, gathered up my purse, and clipped Sherlock's lightweight leash onto his harness. I'd harness trained him as a kitten, so he could be trusted to behave himself outdoors and not try to run off. He looked up at me, his head cocked in question.

I informed him of our plans. "We're going to see Silly."

Hearing the name of his favorite furry friend was all it took for him to drag me to the door. With the force nearly pulling my shoulder from the socket, you'd think he was an eighty-pound mastiff, not an eight-pound kitty-cat. He pawed eagerly at the edge of the door and looked up at me, chirping, his whiskers twisting with impatience.

A grin claimed my lips. "I'm going as fast as I can, boy."

I opened the door, we stepped out into the hall, and I turned to lock the door behind us. With Sherlock trotting ahead of me, I made my way down the narrow staircase that led from our attic space to the second floor of the house. This floor had been converted into two one-bedroom apartments, both leased by women in their fifties. From the second-floor landing, Sherlock led me down the wide, curving staircase to the foyer on the first floor. The first-floor unit was much larger, a two-bedroom model that served as home for a professional couple in their mid-thirties who worked long hours and were rarely home to enjoy their beautiful space.

Sherlock and I exited onto the porch. It was a sunny late-spring day, the trees and flowers in fresh bloom. We flounced down the steps and circled through the opening in the white picket fence. While our home was painted a cheery robin's egg blue with white trim, the house next door was decidedly more feminine. Ballet-slipper pink paint coated the exterior, with the railings and shutters painted a darker dusty rose, the perfect color scheme for its current inhabitant.

Sherlock and I walked past the white SUV in the driveway. A decal adhered to each side read HOUSE CALLS HOME HEALTH SERVICE in red lettering. The vehicle was here every weekday afternoon around this same time, so I paid it little mind. An older model silver minivan sat in front of the house, too. The van had seen better days. One of the hubcaps was missing, and a rounded dent in the back bumper evidenced the driver having backed into something, probably a pole. The van had rolled off the assembly line long before backup cameras came standard. My neighbor's lean, lanky housekeeper stood next to the open sliding side door of the van. She wore sneakers, a pair of stretchy black yoga pants, and an oversized T-shirt, clothing that would allow her the freedom of movement she'd need to perform her duties. Her brown hair was pulled up into a high ponytail to keep it out of the way while she cleaned. She wrangled her fancy Dyson vacuum of the van. Though many of her clients probably owned a less expensive plug-in style vacuum, the lightweight cordless model she'd brought with her was likely easier and quicker for her to use. Plus, it came with an assortment of useful attachments and brushes for crevices, curtains, and whatnot, which she carried in a tall, freestanding bag. I could use a nice vac like that to suck up Sherlock's furry dust bunnies, but I'd have to make do with a broom for now. My starving student's budget didn't allow for any luxuries.

Sherlock trotted up the front steps to the porch, his tail swishing in anticipation. I followed him up to the porch. Like many Victorians, this house featured scalloped shingles and decorative gingerbread trim, as well as elegant double doors. A transom filled with a decorated stained-glass panel of pink roses added yet more color and interest over the wide doorframe. The housekeeper came up the steps behind me as I raised a hand and rapped. *Knock-knock.* "It's me!" I called.

Eleanor's voice came from inside. "Come on in, Austen!"

You can probably guess which famous writer I'm named after. My mother is a librarian and rare book dealer who adores the classics, especially those penned by witty and perceptive female writers. Like me, she was fond of things from yesteryear.

I opened the door and held it to allow the housekeeper to carry her vacuum and cleaning supplies inside. Once she'd cleared the threshold, Sherlock and I stepped inside the expansive foyer. A marble floor graced the entry, recently refinished courtesy of yours truly, and a wide staircase curved up from the first floor to the second. Eleanor sprawled on her velvet-covered fainting couch in the parlor to my right, her cane resting across her ribcage. My neighbor had walked the earth for ninety-four years and, though she'd slowed down some, seemed determined to stride the globe for at least another decade. She wore an oversized Gladys Knight concert T-shirt over lightweight denim pants with an elastic waistband, easy-on easy-off clothing she could manage with her arthritis, but a nod to the fun girl she'd once been—and still was. Her pewter hair hung to her shoulders in a sassy shag. She smiled as Sherlock and I walked into the room.

Eleanor's nurse, Bonnie, stood at the open antique rolltop desk, digging around in her black medical bag. Eleanor had suffered a minor stroke three months earlier, and her son had hired a nurse to come by the house to check on his mother Monday through Friday. On the weekends, he came to the house himself to make sure his mother was feeling all right. Finding both the house and its owner to be charming, I spent a lot of time at Eleanor's and had met Bonnie before. She was a seasoned R.N. Her blue scrubs hung loosely over her round body. Her bleached, bobbed hair curved around her face just like the deep laugh lines curved around her mouth. She looked up and nodded in greeting.

I returned Eleanor's smile and Bonnie's nod, and bent down to unclip Sherlock from his leash. The instant he was freed, Eleanor cupped a gnarled hand around her thin lips. "Silly!" she called in a singsong voice. "Your boyfriend is here!"

A stampede sounded on the stairs and Silly—formally Princess Priscilla the Chinchilla Persian—came running down from the upper floor. She careened around the banister, momentum carrying her in a sideways slide across the smooth, freshly polished floor of the foyer. She scrambled for a few seconds, trying to gain purchase. The cat was as beautiful as she was spirited. Hints of silver underlay her snowy white fur, and her gray-blue eyes appeared to be outlined with thick black eyeliner. Despite her purebred pedigree, she behaved with little civility or decorum. She was as wild as an alley cat, especially if she'd gotten into Eleanor's stash of catnip. After finally gaining traction, Silly rushed Sherlock and tackled him to the rug which, like her, was Persian. Though both cats were around five years in age, they behaved like kittens around each other, enjoying rough-and-tumble play.

Bonnie found what she'd been digging for and pulled a digital blood-pressure cuff from her bag. While the two cats wrestled as harmlessly as the choreographed routines of their counterparts in the WWE, Bonnie launched into her own routine. First, she wrapped the blood pressure cuff around Eleanor's bony arm, activated it, and checked the readout. "One-ten over seventy," she reported. "Good." She aimed a thermometer at Eleanor's forehead to check her temperature. "Ninety-eight point six." She held out a small device and Eleanor slid her finger into it. "Your oxygen level is good, too." Bonnie returned the pulse oximeter to her bag and directed Eleanor to follow with her eyes as she moved her index finger from one side to the other in front of the elderly woman. "Perfect. You're going to outlive us all."

Eleanor grinned mischievously. "You want to know the secret to living a long life?"

Bonnie cocked her head. "Good clean living? A daily walk? Eating lots of vegetables?"

Eleanor waved a dismissive hand and issued a *pshaw*. "If you want to live a long time, toss back a shot of bourbon just before bedtime."

Bonnie shook both her head and a finger. "Eleanor Potter. You should be ashamed of yourself."

The old woman snorted. "My mama told me the same thing dozens of times, but I never was. I was having too much fun to feel any shame over it." Eleanor tucked her hair behind her ears, revealing a pair of emerald teardrop earrings hanging from her lobes.

Bonnie eyed the jewels. "Your earrings are gorgeous."

They certainly were. They must be worth a small fortune, too. Eleanor didn't wear costume jewelry. Her skin reacted poorly to cheap metals.

"Thanks." Eleanor reached up a hand to finger the jewels and beamed. "I normally only wear them on special occasions but, with my husband gone ten years and me barely able to get around, who knows how many more big events I'll attend? I've decided that every day I have left is a special occasion."

Bonnie nodded in agreement. "That's a good philosophy."

Eleanor went on. "My mother originally bought these earrings to wear to South Carolina in nineteen forty-eight. She and my father drove up there to see Harry Truman on his Whistlestop Tour. Took me with them."

"That must've been so exciting," I said.

Eleanor shrugged. "It was so crowded we couldn't see anything but the back of the people in front of us. I climbed up a light post to get a better look but my mother scolded me and made me get down. Apparently 'proper young ladies don't climb poles.'" She made air quotes with her fingers.

Whirr! The sound of the vacuum starting upstairs caused Silly to spring from the skirmish on the rug and bolt under the fainting couch. *Such melodrama.* The expensive vac was among the quietest on the market.

Eleanor leaned over to look underneath the furniture. "Quit being silly, Silly! You've heard that sound a thousand times before."

The volume of the vacuum decreased to a mere whisper of white noise a few seconds later. The maid must have closed the door to whichever room she was tending to.

Returning to the business at hand, Bonnie pulled a plastic pill box from her bag, opened the compartment marked FRIDAY, and dumped the three pills into a plastic cup. She reached out a hand to help Eleanor sit up straight and handed her the cup. Eleanor tossed back the pills, then took the cup of water her nurse offered to wash them down.

As Bonnie packed her things back into her bag, Eleanor used her cane to lever herself up from her couch. "Got a fun weekend planned, Bonnie?"

"Sure do." Bonnie zipped her bag closed and slung it over her shoulder. "My daughters and grandkids are taking me out to dinner to celebrate my birthday."

"How fun!" Eleanor said. "How many does this make, if you don't mind me asking?"

"Sixty-five," Bonnie said.

"Sixty-five?" A cloud passed over Eleanor's face. "Does that mean you'll be retiring soon?"

Bonnie barked a laugh. "If only! My no-good husband ran off, and left me and our three girls when I was only twenty-seven. He never stuck with a job long enough for me to catch up with him and collect child support. Had to raise and support the girls all by myself. I haven't managed to save much for retirement. Seemed it was always something. Braces for the kids. A new water heater. A car repair. Spent my whole life living paycheck to paycheck."

Eleanor offered a sympathetic smile. "I'm glad you'll still be my nurse, but I'm sorry to hear you've struggled."

Bonnie shrugged. "It wasn't easy, but I count my blessings. We always had food on the table and a roof over our heads. It could've been worse."

"That's the spirit."

Her visit complete, Bonnie walked to the door with her usual rolling gait. Eleanor hobbled along after her and held the door. "Thanks for coming, Bonnie. See you on Monday. Enjoy your birthday!"

The grandfather clock looming in the corner chimed the hour. *Donggg. Donggg.*

Eleanor glanced at the clock and looked my way. "The vet's expecting us soon. We'd better round up Silly."

She might have said *we*, but we both knew she meant *me*. She'd have no chance of catching her rambunctious cat on her own. I went to the foyer, retrieved Silly's plastic carrier from the coat closet, and placed it open on the floor. The vacuum had stopped upstairs, so I didn't have the sound to cover my footsteps. I tiptoed back to the parlor. With any luck, the cats wouldn't notice me approaching. They'd tired of wrangling, and now lay on the rug licking each other's cheeks and foreheads. I averted my eyes, hoping Silly wouldn't realize I was coming for her. No such luck. She spotted me coming in her direction, surmised my devious intentions, and leapt to her four feet, bolting for the kitchen and leaving both Sherlock and me in her dust. *Dang it!*

I dashed after the cat, but I wasn't quick enough. She bounded past the dinette set, ricocheted off the refrigerator, and darted out the other doorway into the hall. By the time I ran into the hallway, she'd fled up the stairs, vacuum be damned.

Eleanor had hobbled after me and stopped me when I was halfway up the stairs. "It's no use chasing her, Austen. She's too fast. You know what we'll have to do."

"I do."

There was only one way we'd get Silly into her carrier. We'd have to break out the catnip. The pretty Persian was positively addicted to the stuff. If she were human, she'd need to attend a twelve-step program—or, since cats had twice as many feet as humans, maybe a twenty-four-step program. My Sherlock was among the minority of cats who had no reaction to the substance. Perhaps he'd inherited some type of immunity from his feline ancestors.

Eleanor retrieved the shiny antique silver snuff box from atop the piano in her parlor and carried it over to Silly's carrier. She pried the lid open, reached in to retrieve a large pinch of the dried herb, and tossed it atop the soft blanket lining the bottom of the carrier. In case the single pinch wasn't enough, she repeated the procedure, adding another toss of catnip. A fresh smell filled the air, like dried grass with a hint of lemon and mint.

While dogs were best known for having an enhanced sense of smell, cats were certainly no shirks when it came to their sniffers. Silly promptly appeared at the top of the stairs, her nose raised and twitching, her whiskers vibrating. Eleanor and I exchanged knowing looks. The cat wouldn't be able to resist. Sure enough, Silly trotted down the stairs, raised her nose again, and turned to look at her carrier. She eyed me and Eleanor, giving us dirty looks. She knew the carrier meant temporary captivity and a trip to the doctor who would poke her with needles and force her to endure certain other humiliations, but she simply couldn't resist the siren scent of the catnip. She strode zombielike to the carrier as if hypnotized, stepped inside, and dropped onto her side, rubbing herself against the blanket as if it were her long-lost lover. Catnip mimicked feline sex hormones, after all. That's what made it so irresistible. Before Silly could come to her senses, so to speak, I rushed over and closed the door to her carrier.

Eleanor pumped a fist. "Good work, Austen! You've earned a cookie when we get back."

I admonished Sherlock to behave himself while we were gone, and grabbed the handle to lift Silly's carrier. Eleanor cupped her hand around her mouth and called up to her housekeeper. "We're leaving, Courtney! Be sure to lock up when you go!"

A disembodied voice came from above. "I will, Mrs. Potter!"

Eleanor followed me and her cat out the door, making sure to lock it tight behind us. We continued on to my blue Nissan Versa. I'd bought the car used with savings from the part-time job I'd held during high school and a little help from my parents. It was a small, fuel-efficient car, perfect for getting from my apartment to my classes and around town without cutting too much into my meager budget.

As we rolled to a stop at our first traffic sign, my eyes spotted a sign affixed to the light post. A French bulldog name Pierre had gone missing last week. His owner's phone number appeared on the flyer, along with a color photo of the dog, who was utterly adorable. The information stated that he was a blue merle, and his coat was a light gray. His eyes were grayish blue, much like Silly's. Pierre's eyes seemed to lock on mine and I felt a tug at my heart. I couldn't even imagine how worried I'd be if my precious Sherlock ever went missing. I hoped Pierre would turn up soon.

We drove on to the vet's office two miles away. The parking lot was crowded. I cruised slowly through until coming across an open space at the far end. I pulled into the space and eased up to the car facing us, a small Mitsubishi in a yellow-gold color that fell somewhere between school bus and processed cheese. Two sporty red stripes spanned the grill. After helping Eleanor out of the passenger seat, I rounded up Silly's carrier from the back. Her lustful writhing had declined as she'd acclimated to the catnip, and she now settled for rubbing only her cheek against the blanket. Carefully carrying the cat so as not to jostle her, I followed my neighbor into the office.

A thirtyish dark-haired receptionist sat at the counter, working her keyboard and staring at her computer screen through round tortoiseshell glasses. I recognized her from my visit to the office with Sherlock a few weeks earlier, when Doctor Burgess had administered a rabies booster and other routine vaccinations. Her name tag read Felicity, a fitting name given that she seemed to wear a perpetual smile, a plus for front-end staff. As Eleanor shuffled her way to the counter, the woman glanced up. "Hi, there! Gimme just one second to finish entering this data." She spent a few more seconds typing, then hit the enter key with a flourish. "Done." She returned her attention to Eleanor with an expectant lift of her brows. "How may I help you?"

Eleanor used her cane like a pointer to indicate the carrier in my hands. "Princess Priscilla has a two-thirty appointment for her annual checkup."

"Okey doke." Felicity worked her keyboard and mouse again before turning back to Eleanor. "She's all checked in. You can take a seat. A tech will be right with you."

"Thanks."

Eleanor and I slid into adjacent vinyl-covered chairs with Silly's carrier at our feet. I glanced around the room at the pets waiting to see the doctor. A beagle puppy wriggled in a woman's arms. A black lab mix wearing a plastic cone of shame around his neck sat on his haunches, panting softly. A skinny Siamese cat mewed incessantly from inside a soft-sided carrier, demanding answers for his unjust imprisonment. *Mew? Mew? Mew?* Maybe his owner should try a little catnip, too. It might make him more compliant.

A community bulletin board hung on the side wall. The flyer for the missing French bulldog was posted there, along with one for a missing miniature Pomeranian named Itsy-Bitsy. Itsy-Bitsy's owner had offered a reward of five-hundred dollars for her safe return. While the purebred dogs sure were cute, I knew pet overpopulation was a big problem. I'd adopted Sherlock from the city animal shelter rather than buying him from a breeder. Although Silly was a purebred Persian, Eleanor had adopted her from a rescue group after a breeder decided to get out of the business and didn't want to keep the cat as a pet. Seemed pretty heartless to me. Cats were sentient creatures, not mere business equipment, but the breeder didn't seem to see it that way. I was glad Silly had found a new, loving home with my neighbor.

An auburn-haired, freckle-faced vet tech emerged from the back room and glanced around, her gaze stopping on Silly's crate. "Princess Priscilla Potter?"

"That's us." Eleanor put her hands on the armrests and pushed herself to a stand before rounding up her cane.

I stood and picked up the carrier.

The tech's nose wriggled. "Is that catnip I smell?"

"Sure is," Eleanor said. "We'd have never got Silly into her carrier without it. She's as stubborn as they come."

The tech chuckled. My neighbor and I followed the woman back to an examination room, where I set Silly's carrier atop the table.

The tech walked over to a computer on a countertop and ran through a series of preliminary questions about the patient. "Is she eating and drinking normally?"

"Yep," Eleanor said. "No problems."

"Normal bowel movements?"

"Yep. Regular as clockwork."

After asking a few more questions, the tech pulled Silly from the carrier to get her weight. She sat her on the small scale and eyed the readout. "She's gained a pound since last year. You'll have to cut back on her treats."

Silly growled as if she'd understood— *Rrrowl!*—and the three of us shared a laugh.

The tech held the cat still with a crooked arm, while gently inserting a plastic stool collection stick into her backside. Silly's eyes went wide and she hissed in indignation, but after a quick twist the stick was removed and the cat was released. She swished her tail and glared at the tech. *If looks could kill...*

There was a soft knock at the door and the veterinarian entered. Dr. Burgess was a middle-aged dark-skinned man with a balding head and a professional yet personable demeanor. "Hello, Mrs. Potter. Good to see you and Princess Priscilla. I trust you both are doing well?"

Eleanor dipped her head in acknowledgment. "I had a checkup myself just an hour ago. Luckily for me, my nurse didn't put a stick in my rear to take a stool sample."

Amusement crinkled the doctor's eyes. "Let's have a look." He lifted Silly's gums to take a look at her teeth, shined a light in her eyes, held a stethoscope to her chest to listen to her heart, and put a hand underneath her furry belly, groping along her abdomen. When he finished, he released her and stepped back. "She appears to be the picture of health. I'll do a quick blood draw so the lab can run the usual tests."

"Eek!" Eleanor's grip tightened on her cane and she put her free hand over her eyes. "I can't watch."

The vet tech held Silly down while the doctor quickly drew the blood. Silly growled in protest, but the procedure was over before she could put up a fight. The doc stepped away from the table with the vial of blood. "All clear. You can look now."

Eleanor peeked through her fingers. On seeing that her cat appeared annoyed but otherwise unaffected, she exhaled in relief. The exam complete, the tech slid Silly back into her carrier. The doc stepped into the hall and held the door, bidding us goodbye as we left.

"Thanks, Doc!" Eleanor said. "Silly and I will see you next year."

He gave her a smile. "I'll be looking forward to it."

Chapter Two

We left the room and returned to the foyer. I set the carrier atop the counter as Eleanor settled her tab with the receptionist. Silly turned circles inside. Stray bits of catnip fell out onto the desk, but a few tiny dried leaves were nothing to fret over. The vet's staff dealt with much worse messes on a regular basis. In fact, a nervous yorkie had left a fresh puddle of piddle under a chair just now. After handing Eleanor her receipt, the receptionist used her hand to brush the catnip from the counter, then stood to round up a roll of paper towels and a spray bottle of disinfectant to clean the floor.

Eleanor, Silly, and I made our way out to the car and headed home. On the drive, I spotted yet another sign for a missing dog. Like the others, this pet was purebred, a Cavalier King Charles Spaniel who went by the name Chucky. *Odd how many dogs are missing from the area.*

We arrived back at Eleanor's house to see Sherlock lying atop the upright piano in her front window, keeping an eye on the street, as always, a self-appointed watchman. I carried Silly inside and the two cats instantly resumed their play, chasing each other up the stairs, then back down again.

Eleanor reached into her purse, pulled out a twenty-dollar bill, and held it out to me. "Here you go. For the taxi service."

I raised a palm. "You don't owe me anything. I'm happy to help a friend."

She gave me a smile. "That's sweet of you to say, Austen. Most of my friends have passed on. It's nice to know I've still got at least one." She stepped forward and embraced me in a warm hug. When she released me, she motioned for me to follow her to the kitchen. "Let's get you that cookie."

"Just one?" I teased. "That doesn't seem fair."

Sherlock enjoyed another few minutes of play with his buddy, while I sat at the kitchen table with Eleanor and enjoyed a cup of hot tea and two of her scrumptious oatmeal raisin cookies. She added a dash of nutmeg to the recipe, and the spice made all the difference.

When I finished, I washed my teacup at the sink and said, "I'd better get back to my studies."

"You'll ace that exam," Eleanor said. "You always do."

It was true. I had a straight-A average. I loved my studies and worked hard to make sure I got the most out of each course.

I went into the foyer in search of my cat. "Sherlock!" I called. "Where did you go?"

He peeked his head through the balusters on the banister at the top of the stairs and looked down at me. Silly stuck her head out a few balusters over.

I patted my leg. "Come here, boy! It's time to go!"

My cat made no move to come down the steps. The stubborn kitty drove a hard bargain. "Will you come down for a tuna treat?"

That promise did the trick. Sherlock traipsed down the stairs and allowed me to attach his harness and leash. Eleanor and Silly walked us to the door. I wished my neighbor a good weekend, and she returned the sentiment. Silly gave Sherlock one last lick across the cheek, a goodbye kiss. My cat and I returned home, where I promptly gave him the treat I'd promised.

* * *

I spent most of Saturday hitting the books. While I studied, Sherlock stared out the window, surveilling the street. Late that afternoon, he chirped and twitched his whiskers. I leaned over and peeked out the glass to see Silly pacing on a windowsill in a second-floor guest room next door. She looked up at Sherlock, batted her beautiful eyes, and swished her bushy tail. *Flirty feline.*

I continued cramming for my exam on Sunday, though I took a break to walk Sherlock through the nearby squares on his leash. He enjoyed sniffing the plants, watching the people and birds, using a tree trunk as a scratching post. Though most of the residents were by now used to seeing me and Sherlock strolling about, one of the tourists expressed surprise. "Is that a cat on a leash?" She proceeded to answer her own question. "It is! It's a cat on a leash!"

My dedication and determination paid off. Monday's exam went well, and I felt confident I'd earned a near-perfect score. *Yay, me!*

The rest of the week passed by with no surprises, but Friday morning brought big trouble. I was sitting at the table in my apartment, sipping my coffee and reading about the role of government in historic preservation, when Sherlock rose to a rigid crouch at the window. He chattered at something outside and stared downward with laser focus, slapping his tail against the glass in irritation. *Whap-whap-whap.*

"What's go you so worked up, boy?" I stood and walked over to the window. Bonnie's white SUV was parked in Eleanor's driveway next door. The doors bore the familiar red logo for HOUSE CALLS HOME HEALTH SERVICE. The words were easily readable, even from three stories up. Funny I'd never noticed the especially large size of the lettering. And what was the SUV doing here in the middle of the morning? Bonnie always came in the early afternoon. *Could Eleanor be sick? Did she call the agency and ask them to send a nurse by?*

Below, a woman sporting a blond bob and wearing scrubs exited Eleanor's house. She walked down the pathway from the front porch of Eleanor's house to the driveway, aiming for the SUV. Although the bobbed blonde hair said the woman was Bonnie, she didn't move with the nurse's normal rolling gait. Rather, she proceeded in fast, long strides. *She must be in a hurry today.* She carried her usual black nylon bag but, rather than holding the short straps in her hand, she cradled it under her arm like an oversized football. She struggled to hold it. The items inside seemed to be shifting.

Sherlock's lips spread in a hiss and he put his paws to the window, clawing desperately at the glass as if trying to tear through it. He cast a look my way, as if imploring me to act. *Something's not right. Had Sherlock seen something?*

I grabbed my cell phone, tucked it into the back pocket of my jeans, and hurried out of my apartment. My sneakers pounded on the stairs. There seemed to be twice as many steps today. I reached the second-floor landing and swung myself around the newel post to launch myself down the next flight. As soon as my feet hit the first-floor landing, I rushed the door, throwing it open. I emerged onto the porch just in time to see the white SUV back out of Eleanor's driveway. The dappled sunlight reflected off the windshield, making it difficult to see inside. I raised an arm and waved. "Bonnie! Wait!"

Rather than stop, the SUV turned to head in the opposite direction and took off so fast the tires squealed. *Screeee!* The rapid departure seemed strange. Bonnie usually drove carefully. *Had she not seen me waving?*

I ran down the steps and hightailed it to Eleanor's door. To my surprise, the door stood open a few inches. In her haste, Bonnie must have forgotten to close it behind her.

I opened the door and stuck my head inside. "Eleanor?" I called. "Eleanor?"

No response came. A sick feeling slithered into my gut. I called her name again. Still nothing.

I stepped into the foyer and glanced around. *There she is.* My elderly neighbor lay on her fainting couch. Her eyes were closed. Her head lolled to one side and her jaw hung slack. *Oh, no!*

Fearing the worst, I dashed over and dropped to my knees on the rug. "Eleanor?" I reached out and gently shook her shoulder. She didn't respond. I put a hand to her neck to feel for a pulse, noting that she wasn't wearing her favorite emerald teardrop earrings today. Though I felt a throb, my heart pounded so hard in terror I couldn't be sure whether the pulse was hers or my own. I pulled my hand back and leaned in to take a closer look. The big blue vein on the side of her neck slowly vibrated. My gaze moved to her chest. It rose and fell just barely as she took shallow breaths. *She's alive! Thank goodness!* Unfortunately, my relief was fleeting. Eleanor might be alive, but she was unconscious. *Has she suffered another stroke? Why in the world would Bonnie leave her like this?*

When I tried again to rouse Eleanor with no success, I whipped my phone from my pocket and dialed 9-1-1. "Send an ambulance right away!" I rattled off the address and gave the dispatcher the basic details. *Elderly woman. Non-responsive. No clear evidence of trauma.* I ran out onto the porch so I could flag down the first responders. Though I hadn't seen Silly when I'd gone inside, I made sure to close the door behind me so she couldn't attempt an escape if she came to the foyer.

Though it was less than two minutes before my ears

detected the *woo-woo-woo* of an approaching ambulance, it felt like an eternity. I walked halfway down the front steps and waved my arms over my head. "Here!" I cried, though there was no way the paramedics could hear me from inside the vehicle. "Here!"

They pulled to a stop and I rushed to the curb as the bay doors swung open. Two paramedics slid out, one male, one female. The woman asked some quick questions as she grabbed her bag and her partner lowered the gurney. "Any idea what happened?"

"None," I said. "I just came over and found her unconscious."

I led them inside, closed the door behind us, and stood back as they tended to Eleanor. They took her vitals with practiced efficiency. The female EMT continued to question me as they worked. "Any idea when she last ate?"

"She wakes up early, around six. She normally has a cup of black coffee and oatmeal for breakfast." I knew her routine because I'd helped out after her stroke, making sure she ate and kept up her strength.

"Is she on any medications?"

"Several," I said, "but I have no idea which ones or in what dosages. She had a minor stroke a few months back. Her home health nurse administers them. Her name's Bonnie. She works for House Calls Home Health Service. I saw her leaving right before I came over."

The woman's brow furrowed. "Her nurse was just here?"

"Yes. She left in a hurry."

"Who's Mrs. Potter's doctor?"

"I'm not sure. Her son would know. I'll call him." As I dialed Eleanor's son from my cell phone, the male paramedic cracked open a smelling salt packet and held it under Eleanor's nose. Though my neighbor failed to respond, my nose involuntarily crinkled as the stench of ammonia filled my nostrils.

Eleanor's son answered my call right away and I filled him in. "I don't know what happened. Her nurse came by early today. I saw her car through my window. I thought maybe your mother wasn't feeling well so I came over to check on her. I found the front door open and your mother unconscious on the couch."

His voice rose an octave in outrage. "Bonnie just left Mom lying there?"

"It looks that way. Paramedics are here. They need to know who her doctor is."

He gave me the doctor's name and asked me to find out where the ambulance would be taking his mother. I consulted the paramedics and repeated what they told me. "Memorial Hospital."

"I'm on my way."

The paramedics carefully loaded Eleanor onto the gurney and carried her out to the ambulance. As the driver reactivated the siren and the ambulance pulled away from the curb, I turned back to the house. *I should lock up.* I scrambled up to my apartment to grab the spare key to Eleanor's house. Her son had given me the key when she'd been in the hospital after her stroke. I'd taken care of Silly, watered her plants, and brought in her mail until she'd recovered enough to return home. When I'd attempted to return the key to Eleanor, she'd suggested I keep the key in case of an emergency. *Good thing I still have it.*

I opened my door to find Sherlock pacing back and forth in front of the window. The loud sound of the siren must have upset him. I ran a hand over his head. "It's okay, boy. I'll be right back."

I left him again and scurried over to Eleanor's house. As I went to lock her front door from the outside, it struck me that I'd better check on Silly. She hadn't come around while the paramedics had been in the house. I supposed she might have been frightened by the sound of the siren, as well as the strangers in her home, but Silly wasn't normally a 'fraidy cat. Like Sherlock, she tended to be more curious and often threw caution to the wind.

I stepped inside and closed the door behind me. "Silly?" I called. "Where are you, girl?" I waited for a moment, but the cat didn't come. I ventured into the parlor and looked around. I even got down on my hands and knees to peer under the fainting couch and bookshelves. *No cat in here.*

"Silly?" I called again as I strode through the dining room. Still no sign of her. I walked to the kitchen. No cat. *Hmm.* Wherever Silly was in the house, the sound of the can opener would bring her running. I walked over to the counter and pushed down on the arm to activate it. *Rrrrrrr.* I released the lever and listened, but heard no tell-tale sounds of paws trotting down the stairs. *Could she be shut in a closet or cabinet?*

I opened the pantry and every cabinet in the kitchen. There was no sign of the cat. I even tried the fridge and freezer, just to be thorough. She wasn't there, either. Nor was she in the coat closet.

"Silly?" I called again to no avail. Though I hated to invade Eleanor's privacy, I knew the woman would want me to ensure that her cat was safe and sound. I pushed open the door to Eleanor's bedroom and gasped. *No!* The drawers to her dresser hung open, the contents tossed about the room. Slips. Socks. Nightgowns. Bras. A half dozen pairs of plain white granny panties.

The jewelry box atop the dresser had been turned over, the contents spread out across the surface. I rushed over to take a look. Only cheap costume jewelry remained. Someone had picked through the pieces, taking the items of value. *Had that someone been Bonnie?* Though all evidence pointed to the woman, I could hardly believe it. She'd seemed so caring and trustworthy. Then again, she had taken note of Eleanor's emerald earrings last week. I remembered her complimenting my neighbor on them. *Had she taken them off Eleanor's ears earlier while the woman lay unconscious?*

I whipped out my phone and dialed 9-1-1 for the second time that day. "My neighbor's been robbed." I ran through the details—who I was, why I was at the house, what I'd discovered. "Her bedroom has been ransacked. It looks like the thief took some jewelry."

My heart broke at the thought of how violated and unsafe Eleanor would feel when she learned her home had been robbed—assuming my neighbor and friend came home at all. *What if she never recovers?*

I continued to search for Silly as I waited for the police to arrive. Though I looked high, low, and everywhere in between, I had no luck. But I had an ace in the hole. *Catnip.*

I retrieved the antique snuff box, opened it, and grabbed a large pinch of the stuff. I tossed it onto the Persian rug. Eleanor wouldn't mind. It could easily be vacuumed up, and she'd appreciate me ensuring that Silly was safe. I walked to the foyer and waved my hand over the open snuff box, sending the scent wafting through the air. Still no cat.

Wherever Silly was hiding in the house, the catnip should draw her out. I carried the snuff box into every room, dropping a pinch onto the floor in each space, to no avail. *Where did she go?*

My stomach twisted itself into a tight knot. *Could Silly have slipped out the open door as Bonnie left?* The thought that Princess Priscilla could be lost forever was far worse than the loss of mere possessions. Property could be replaced but, if her precious kitty disappeared, Eleanor would never recover from her broken heart.

Chapter Three

A half hour later, a policeman arrived. He was a seasoned cop, around forty or so, with broad shoulders, tan skin, and dark hair streaked with silver. His name badge read M. Lorenzo. After introducing himself, he said, "I understand you called to report a burglary?"

"That's correct." I told Officer Lorenzo everything that had happened that day. How Sherlock had acted antsy at the window of our apartment, drawing my attention to the white SUV in the driveway and the woman in scrubs leaving with the black bag. How I'd found the front door open and my elderly neighbor unconscious on her couch. How she'd been taken away in an ambulance. How I'd returned to lock the place up and discovered that her bedroom had been ransacked. "Her cat is missing, too. She's a purebred chinchilla Persian."

After Officer Lorenzo took some quick notes, I led him upstairs to Eleanor's bedroom so he could take a look for himself. He frowned on seeing the mess.

"Eleanor's nurse commented on her emerald earrings last week," I said. "They appear to be missing now. They were teardrop earrings in a gold setting."

"You got a phone number for the nurse?"

"No," I said, "but I'm sure Eleanor's son does. I can give you his number." I was just about to rattle off the number, when a knock sounded at Eleanor's front door. We made our way downstairs. I opened the door. There stood Bonnie dressed in a pair of blue scrubs. *Huh?*

She offered a smile. "Hi, Austen." The smile faltered when she spotted the policeman standing behind me. Worry creased her forehead. "Everything okay?" Her gaze darted about, as if she were looking for her patient.

"Okay?" I repeated. "Not at all. Why did you leave Eleanor earlier?'

The worry crease deepened and confusion puckered her face. "Leave Eleanor?" She cocked her head. "What are you talking about?"

The policeman stepped forward. "Let's all talk on the porch."

We made our way outside. I told Bonnie that I'd come over to check on Eleanor after I'd seen her SUV at the house earlier. "I saw you come out of the house with your bag under your arm. I waved to try to stop you, but you drove off."

Bonnie shook her head. "That wasn't me or my car. Eleanor's on my afternoon schedule. I haven't been by here yet today."

Now it was my turn to feel confused. Though the SUV had looked like Bonnie's, the logo on the side had seemed larger than I recalled, larger than that on the SUV parked in the driveway now. The woman I'd seen hadn't moved like Bonnie, either. She'd also been wearing glasses.

Before I could say anything more, Bonnie gestured to the house. "Is Eleanor okay?"

"No," I said. "She's at the hospital. Her door was open when I came over and I found her on her couch, non-responsive."

"Oh, no!" She reflexively covered her mouth with her hand. "I hope she'll be okay."

The officer eyed Bonnie. "Where were you earlier?'

"I've been making house calls all morning." She opened her bag and pulled out a small notebook organizer. She flipped it open to show him her schedule for the day. "See? I've made five calls already."

He gestured to the schedule. "I'll need contact information for your patients."

"Of course," she said. "They'll vouch for me. I can show you my mileage log, too, if that will clear me." She turned my way, her expression still worried, but also hurt, insulted, and angry. "You know I'd never hurt Eleanor. She's my favorite patient!"

I had no idea what to say. I saw what I saw, but what, exactly, had I seen? My impression had been that the woman was Bonnie, but maybe that was simply because she'd resembled the nurse. I could have been mistaken, about both the person and the vehicle. I hedged my bets. "I'm sure Officer Lorenzo will get things sorted out."

While the policeman finished questioning Bonnie and dusted for fingerprints inside, I returned to my apartment and drafted a missing cat flyer for Silly. I had dozens of pics of her on my cell phone. I included a close-up photo that showed her sweet face. I asked anyone who'd seen her to call my phone number. I printed out a dozen color copies.

Officer Lorenzo called my cell to let me know he'd finished gathering evidence. I returned to Eleanor's house to lock up.

He met me on the porch. "I'll notify local pawn shops to keep an eye out for the emerald teardrop earrings. Once we know how things play out with Mrs. Potter, I'll have her or her son identify what other items of jewelry are missing."

I bit my lip and gave him a nod. After Officer Lorenzo left, I locked up Eleanor's house and walked about the neighborhood, posting the missing cat flyers on light posts. As I moved about, I kept an eye out for Silly, looking behind bushes, under parked cars, and up in the trees. She seemed to have vanished into thin air.

As I went to post a flyer, my cell phone rang. The readout on the screen told me it was Bonnie's son calling. I tapped the icon to accept the call and, without preamble, asked, "How is she?"

"She's coming around," he said.

"Thank goodness!" My shoulders finally came down from my ears, but only partly. Silly was still missing, after all.

"They ran a blood screen. It showed a large quantity of a drug called gabapentin in her system. The ER doctor told me it's used to control seizures and for pain relief."

"Did she take too much?"

"Any of it was too much," he said. "It's not one of her usual meds. The only thing I can figure is that there was some sort of mix-up and Bonnie inadvertently gave her a drug intended for another one of her patients."

"Bonnie came by after your mother was taken away. I was looking for Silly and discovered that your mother's bedroom had been ransacked."

"What?!"

I hated to upset him further, but he had a right to know. "It looks like someone might have stolen jewelry. I called the police. Bonnie showed up while the officer was checking things out. She claimed she hadn't come by your mother's house earlier, that she'd been on other house calls all morning."

"Well, if it wasn't her who came by," he said, "then who was it?"

Who, indeed. If the person I saw hadn't been Bonnie, it had been someone who'd gone to quite a bit of effort to look like the woman.

"The officer dusted for fingerprints. If the robber has been arrested before, maybe he'll get a hit. He wants to talk to Eleanor, get an inventory of the missing items."

"Did they take anything besides jewelry?" he asked.

"Not that I noticed." I swallowed the lump of raw emotion in my throat. "But Silly is missing. I've looked everywhere. I'm posting flyers now."

"Oh, no." He released a long breath. "The overdose didn't kill Mom, but losing that cat just might."

I feared the same. "When will she be released?"

"They want to keep her under observation for a few hours. She'll be home tonight. In case Silly shows up, I'm not going to tell her yet that the cat is missing."

"I'll continue to keep an eye out in case she comes back."

"Thanks, Austen."

We ended the call, and I returned my attention to the flyer. The one for the missing Pomeranian had been taped to the same light post days before, the print beginning to fade from the sun. Looked like the furry little pooch was still unaccounted for. I posted my flyer underneath it, closed my eyes, and sent up a quick prayer for the safe return of all of the missing pets.

Chapter Four

Eleanor had burst into tears when I'd given her the sad and scary news that Silly was nowhere to be found. She sat on her porch day after day, waiting and watching for her beloved cat to come home, but her efforts so far had been in vain. Eleanor told Officer Lorenzo that a nurse with a similar hairstyle to Bonnie's had come to her house, claiming to be filling in because Bonnie had purportedly been in a fender bender and wouldn't be able to make her appointments that day. She'd given Eleanor three white tablets that she claimed were calcium tablets recommended by her doctor based on recent communications with him. My trusting neighbor had downed the pills, no questions asked. Of course, the pills turned out to be the gabapentin the ER physician had later discovered in her bloodstream. Eleanor identified several missing items of jewelry, in addition to the emerald teardrop earrings that had been snatched right off her lobes, but none of the pieces appeared at any pawn shops in the area or for sale online that any of us could find.

Despite the best efforts of Officer Lorenzo, no progress

was made on the assault and robbery case over the next few of days. The only fingerprints on Eleanor's jewelry box had been her own. The robber must have worn gloves. Although one neighbor had a security camera with a wide enough range to capture the SUV on the street the day of the incident, the driver had removed the license plates from the vehicle. Without them, it was untraceable. There were hundreds of such vehicles in Savannah and the surrounding region.

Bonnie was cleared. Even before Eleanor was released from the hospital and told Lorenzo that the woman who'd come to her house wasn't Bonnie, her patients had reported that she'd paid them visits the morning of the robbery, just as she'd claimed. There'd be no way Bonnie could have come to Eleanor's, drugged and robbed her, and then made all her appointments across town. What's more, none of Bonnie's patients were on gabapentin. She wasn't on the drug, either. Unless she'd somehow convinced another nurse with access to the drug to provide her with the tablets, it was unclear how she'd even get her hands on the stuff. Officer Lorenzo surmised that someone had been casing Eleanor's house, noticed that Bonnie made regular visits, and disguised themselves as the nurse so that they could gain access and rob the place without raising suspicion. Little did that person know that my cat Sherlock would be watching from our window next door. Lorenzo assumed that either the robber, or someone in the robber's family or circle of friends, had been prescribed the gabapentin that was used to dope Eleanor.

In addition to the flyers I'd posted on the street lights, I posted a missing pet notice on a lost pet site online, as well as on Facebook and other social media, imploring everyone in the neighborhood to keep an eye out for Silly. Sadly, there were no sightings. She didn't return home on her own, either. Eleanor was beside herself, fearing the worst, so fraught with worry that she could hardly eat or sleep. She grew even more frail and feeble. I tried to keep her hopes up, telling her that maybe someone had taken Silly into their home and hadn't yet noticed the flyers or thought to take her to a veterinarian to be scanned for a microchip. "Don't give up yet. Maybe someone will call."

A rainstorm came through the area late the following week, causing both Eleanor and I fresh worry about Silly. Was she somewhere not just lost and alone, but also soaking wet? Silly hated to take baths. She'd be miserable in the rain. What's more, the rain soaked the flyers and made the ink run, ruining them.

As soon as the sun came out, I reprinted flyers and made the rounds again, reposting the flyers. As I was taping one to a post, a thought crept into my mind. The purebred pets were worth a pretty penny. Could the tossed bedroom have been a ruse? Had the robber come to Eleanor's house not for her jewelry, but for her cat? Had the robber resold the animals? I'd heard of animals being stolen by unscrupulous thieves who hoped to collect a reward and, more recently, I'd heard that the same types of cruel individuals were stealing and reselling popular breeds. Could they have targeted Silly and the missing dogs?

I was pondering the situation when the Pomeranian's owner walked up, carrying a new supply of flyers, as well. The woman was fiftyish, with fluffy buff-colored hair not unlike her pet. After introducing myself, I asked, "Can you tell me how your dog disappeared?"

"I let Itsy-Bisty out into the courtyard behind my home. I didn't worry about her being back there because I kept a padlock on the gate. When I went to bring her in a few minutes later, she was gone. The lock was, too, and the gate was open. I'd had some new patio furniture delivered that day, and I must've forgotten to put the lock back on the gate. I must not have closed it well, either. I feel terrible! I should've been more careful. I truly thought I had been." A cloud of guilt passed over her face.

"Nobody's called about her?"

"No. She's microchipped, so I keep hoping I'll hear something. But so far, nothing."

I told the woman about my theory. "Do you think your dog might have been stolen? That someone might have used bolt cutters to remove the lock from your gate?"

Her mouth dropped for a moment, but then closed as her jaw clenched and her eyes flashed in anger. "That would certainly explain things."

"Do you have any security cameras on your home?"

"No. I have a security system, but it's an older model with only an audible alarm if someone breaks in. No cameras."

I pointed to a post across the street, where a flyer for the missing French bulldog still hung. "Your dog and my neighbor's cat aren't the only purebred pets missing. I'm going to do some sleuthing and see what I can find out." I snapped of photo of her flyer so I'd have her phone number. "If I find out anything helpful, I'll be in touch."

"Thanks. My heart is broken. I'd love to get Itsy-Bitsy back."

As I hung the other flyers, I snapped photos of the soggy posts for the King Charles Spaniel and the French bulldog. Fortunately, though the paper was soaked and runny, the phone numbers were still legible.

When I returned home, I phoned the owners to determine the circumstances under which their pets had disappeared.

I spoke first with the owner of the King Charles Spaniel. "My front door has one of those locks with an automated keypad. I came home from work a few weeks back to find my front door partly open. Nothing was missing from my house, though. I'd convinced myself that I must have left the door unlocked and not fully closed when I'd taken out the trash as I left for work that morning, but that would have been very unlike me. Now I'm wondering whether someone watched my house with binoculars and saw me type in the code for my lock. Maybe they obtained the code and opened the door."

"Do you have any security cameras on your house?"

"I do," the man said. "It's one of those doorbell cameras. But on the day my dog disappeared, the morning glories on the trellis beside my door were in bloom. One of the flowers blocked the camera."

Maybe a pet thief had taken advantage of the situation to unlock his door and nab the adorable spaniel. I told him I'd give him a call back if I learned anything that might help him locate his lost pet.

The couple who owned Pierre, the French bulldog, told me that their dog had apparently dug out of their small yard and absconded down the narrow alley behind their home. "He'd never been a digger before, but our security camera showed that he went behind the big metal electric box at the back of our yard. He never came back around. We found a big hole back there. He must've dug it when we weren't looking."

Or maybe someone else had dug the hole from the other side of the fence... They could have lured him through the hole with treats, or even just grabbed him as he came behind the box to investigate.

After we ended the call, I sat back to think. If someone had stolen and resold Silly, it seems that the new owners would want to protect the pet they'd purchased by registering a microchip. Would they assume the pet didn't have one, and have a new one implanted? If so, there'd be no way of tracing the microchip number. Would a vet search for a microchip first before implanting one on a fully-grown pet? I wasn't sure, but I suspected they would. *Hmm.*

I rounded up my laptop and walked over to Eleanor's, where I asked her about Silly's microchip. "Do you have the paperwork from when it was implanted?"

"I sure do," Eleanor said. "I keep all of her vet records." Hobbling along with her cane, she led me to her den, where two tall, old-fashioned wooden filing cabinets flanked an expansive well-polished desk with mahogany inlays. She pulled open the top drawer of one of the filing cabinets, riffled through it, and removed a hanging folder with a hand-lettered tab that read PRINCESS PRISCILLA. She set the file on the desk, took a seat in the posh high-back desk chair, and fingered through the contents. She pulled out a piece of paper and held it out to me. "Here you go."

The document identified the company that maintained the microchip records, and offered their contact information as well as the number on Silly's chip. I placed both the paperwork and my laptop on the desk. After pondering the situation for a moment, I pulled my cell phone from my pocket and called the company. I figured that, for privacy reasons, the company would not reveal the registered owner's name and information. Rather, it was my understanding that, in the event a microchipped pet was found, they would take the caller's information and relay the contact details to the pet's owner. *I might have to fudge a little...*

Eleanor watched me and listened as I dialed the number. Thinking back on the runny phone numbers on the wet flyers, I came up with a story for the representative. "Hi," I said. "I recently re-homed my chinchilla Persian. I promised the new owners that I'd get them copies of her veterinary records. Unfortunately, I spilled a cup of coffee on the slip of paper they gave me with their phone number on it. I think the number has a three in it. But it could be a five? At any rate, I believe the new owners have updated her registry. I don't need their address. I know that's something you have to keep private. But can you provide me with a phone number for them?"

"What's your name?" the representative asked.

"I'm Eleanor Potter," I said.

Eleanor cocked her head and arched a brow.

"And your address?" the woman asked.

I rattled off Eleanor's address.

"And who was your veterinarian?"

"Dr. Burgess."

"Yes. I see that you were the previous registered owner until last week."

A-ha! Someone else had registered the microchip. I was definitely on to something here. *This means Silly is alive and well, doesn't it?*

Seemingly satisfied that I had a legitimate link to the registered pet, she provided a phone number with a 678 area code. *Atlanta.* I knew because I had cousins in the area whose phone numbers began with the same area code. I repeated the number to ensure I'd written it down correctly, thanked the woman, and hung up the phone.

I filled Eleanor in. "Silly must be alive or they wouldn't have updated the registry."

Eleanor clapped her hands in delight, but her happiness was short-lived. A frown claimed her face. "You can't call whoever registered her chip or they might hide Silly. Are you going to call the police?"

Given that the cat had been stolen in one jurisdiction and was now living in another, recovering the cat would take coordination between the two departments. Coordination would take time, and I wanted to get Silly back into Eleanor's arms as soon as possible. *Sometimes you have to take matters into your own paws.* "Let's not call the police just yet. Let's see if we can use this phone number to find the new owner's name and address."

I booted up my computer and clicked to join Eleanor's wifi network. I'd never used my computer at her house before. "What's your password?"

"EleanorLovesSilly," she said. "The first letter of each word is capitalized."

I typed in the password. Once my computer connected to her network, I pulled up a browser and typed in the phone number in quotation marks. I got lucky. The number showed up online in connection with a hairdresser named Layla Zhang. Though the location of her salon was listed online, I could find no home address. *Darn.* But at least we had a place to start.

Eleanor used her cane to raise herself from her chair. "Let's go!"

Atlanta was approximately a four-hour drive from Savannah, and I had a chapter to read in one of my courses, but I wasn't about to tell the woman no. Eleanor had been in a funk since she'd returned home from the hospital the day Silly had been stolen. She shouldn't have to wait another night to see her beloved cat again.

I rounded up my purse from my apartment and gave Sherlock a kiss on the head. "We're going to see about getting Silly back."

On hearing the name of his furry feline friend, Sherlock chirped and looked hopeful. I only hoped we wouldn't disappoint him as well as Eleanor.

I drove to the Salon as fast as I dared. Eleanor kept encouraging me to speed up, but I didn't want to risk getting a speeding ticket. Finally, we reached Atlanta. Using the map app on my phone, we wound our way through traffic to the salon, which was a small shop situated in a strip center between a donut shop and a deli. The bells on the door jingled as Eleanor and I walked inside. The sounds of gossip and a hairdryer set on low greeted us, along with the botanical scents of the shampoos, conditioners, and hairsprays. Five hairdressers moved about their stations as they tended to clients, while four women waited in chairs for their turn. Three of the hairdressers were white, one was black, and one was Asian. All wore flawless makeup and stylish, trendy clothing, making me feel a bit frumpy in my ripped jeans, T-shirt, and sneakers. Given that we were looking for a Layla Zhang, I figured the Asian beautician was likely the woman we were looking for. Nonetheless, we'd come a long way and I figured it couldn't hurt to be sure.

The hairdresser at the closest station turned off the dryer and glanced my way. "Can we help you?"

"I'd like to schedule an appointment with Layla," I said. "A friend recommended her."

The woman turned to the Asian hairdresser in question. Layla put her hands on her client's shoulders and met her gaze in the mirror. "Give me one second." She set her scissors on the stand next to her—a stand on which was displayed a photo of a gorgeous chinchilla Persian. *Silly!*

Eleanor's knuckles turned white on her cane and her brows shot up under her hairline. "It's Silly!" she whispered.

Layla pulled up her schedule on a tablet. She scrolled and scrolled and scrolled. Looking my way, she said, "My soonest open appointment is five months from now." If the woman sitting in her chair now was any indication, I could see why Layla was so booked up. The woman's highlights and lowlights had been impeccably administered, and her cut perfectly complemented her facial features. She named a specific date and time. "Does that work for you?"

"Sure," I said, knowing I'd never make the appointment.

"What's your name?" Layla asked.

"Emma Woodhouse." Emma was a character from a Jane Austen novel, but it was the first name that came to mind.

She repeated the name slowly as she typed it into her tablet. When she finished, she looked up. "Phone number?"

I made one up on the spot, using the 678 prefix.

"Got you down," she said. "See you then."

She'd be seeing me again much sooner than two weeks. She just didn't know it yet.

Chapter Five

Eleanor and I left the salon. It was nearing five o'clock by then, but we had no idea how late the woman intended to work. We parked at the end of the lot where we could wait and follow her when she left. Fortunately, we didn't have to wait long. She called it quits at six.

She exited the salon with her car keys in one hand and a tote bag slung over her shoulder. She climbed into a red Miata convertible, but didn't put the top down. I supposed she didn't want the wind to mess up the hair she'd no doubt spent a significant amount of time properly coiffing.

We heard music key up on her stereo, even though her windows were still rolled up. *Good.* Maybe the loud jams would distract her enough that she wouldn't notice Eleanor and me trailing her.

She took off like a rocket, pulling into the heavy traffic and changing lanes like a pro. I had to zip back and forth to keep up, cringing and offering apologetic waves to the people I'd cut off. After fifteen minutes, she turned into a luxury condominium complex that featured a swimming pool, hot tub, fitness center, and covered parking for residents. The place was gated, but I was able to sneak in behind her by staying right on her bumper. While Layla parked in her reserved spot in the carport, I pulled into a space in the visitor section.

I was afraid she might spot us following her on foot through the parking lot, but once again she was too distracted to notice. She held her cell phone to her ear, giggling coquettishly as she weaved her way through the parked cars and up a set of stairs to a unit on the second floor, with the two of us gaining on her. She stopped at the door marked 2B and said, "Later," into her phone. With that, she slid the phone into her purse, inserted her key into the lock, and opened the door. Only then did she spot our shadows on the wall. She wheeled around in shock, her hand clutched to her chest.

Before Layla could say anything, Silly appeared in the doorway. Eleanor cried out in glee. "Silly!"

The cat launched herself into the air. Eleanor released her cane so that she could catch her beloved pet in her arms. Miraculously, she remained on her feet as Silly rubbed her face under Eleanor's chin as if the woman herself was made of the catnip she so loved. Clearly, the cat had missed her human as much as Eleanor had missed her cat.

When Layla could gather her wits, she said, "What's going on? Why did you follow me home?"

I pointed to Silly. "This cat was stolen. Were you aware of that?"

"Stolen?" Her head jerked back as if evading a slap. "What do you mean? I found her listed online. A rescue group had put her up for adoption."

Adoption? "How much was the adoptions fee?"

"A thousand dollars," Layla said. "The woman I dealt with said that their group needed the funds to save other cats. Not to brag, but I do pretty well. She's such a pretty cat that I was happy to pay the fee and help out."

"Was the woman blond with glasses?"

"She wore glasses, yes," Layla said, "but she had brown hair. Dry, damaged brown hair. She could have really used a deep conditioning treatment." She glanced at Eleanor and Silly. My neighbor was cooing and reassuring her pet, and Silly was purring up a storm in response. Concern and guilt skittered across Layla's face. "I had no idea the cat was stolen or I never would have paid her the money."

I suspected the blond hair on the woman who'd drugged Eleanor had been a wig. "Did the woman give you her name."

"If she did," Layla said, "I don't remember it. It didn't seem important. I was more interested in the cat."

She motioned for Eleanor and me to follow her into her condo. Like its occupant, the space was stylish and classy. Inside, Layla walked over to her breakfast bar and retrieved a computer printout. It was a page from a website for an organization purportedly called Adoptable Orphan Animals. There was a photo of Silly, along with her story, which was surprisingly somewhat accurate. Her bio stated that she'd been abandoned by a breeder when the breeder ceased operations. Her name was listed as Shahbanu, a Persian name that was noted to mean "King's Lady."

Layla said, "I've been calling her 'Sha-sha' as a nickname." She looked from me to Eleanor, and held out a hand, inviting us to take a seat on her sofa. "Tell me exactly what happened."

We sat and gave her the rundown, how Eleanor had been drugged by an as-yet-unidentified woman. How my tabby Sherlock had drawn my attention to the situation by chirping at my window. How the woman who'd stolen the cat had also taken jewelry, perhaps to make the missing cat seem unintentional, a mere unlucky byproduct of a burglary rather than the focus of the theft.

Layla shook her head. "I can't believe it. How can people be so cruel and heartless?"

I'd wondered the same thing. "Do you have a phone number for the woman who brought you the cat?"

"No," she said. "We only communicated via e-mail. I can forward you our messages if you want to take them to the police."

"That would be great."

While she booted up her computer, Eleanor said, "You'll let me take Silly back home, won't you?"

"Of course," Layla said. "I'll miss her, but I could never live with myself if I left you heartbroken. I can get another cat. This time, I'll go in person to the local shelter."

Eleanor reached into her pocketbook and pulled out her checkbook. "I'll reimburse you the money you paid the thief."

Layla waved her hand. "No-no-no. She's yours. I do quite well for myself, as you can probably tell." She motioned about at her tasteful furnishings and art. "I don't need the money. But I would like to stop the thief from taking advantage of people like this ever again. She's done us both wrong. I'd be happy to give the police a statement or whatever you need if you can find her."

But how could we find this woman? "How did she get the cat to you?"

"She brought her here."

"Did you see what kind of car she was driving?"

"No," Layla said, "but this place has security out the wazoo. I can check with the management."

Layla and I left Eleanor and Silly canoodling on the couch and went down to the management office. There, Layla explained our situation to the male security guard, a black man in his late twenties with muscular shoulders the size of bowling balls. He promptly pulled up footage for the day in question. He first showed the recording from the camera mounted over Layla's block of units. Unfortunately, all we could see there was a woman with brown hair and round glasses carrying the cat up to Layla's door. She looked vaguely familiar, but it could be simply that, with brown hair and no makeup, she had an everyday quality.

The security guard showed us the footage from the other cameras, as well. Unfortunately, the woman had entered the property on foot through the management office rather than driving her vehicle into the parking lot. She must have known the cameras would pick up her car and license plate.

I heaved a sigh as we watched her walk away, out of camera range. "I'm not sure where to go from here. I don't know how else we can identify her."

The security guard said, "We can see who owns the domain name for the alleged rescue group."

I gave him a smile. "Smart thinking. Do you know how to do that?"

He scoffed in jest. "Do I know how to do that. Of course, I do." As the footage continued to play, he turned to another computer, made a fist, and blew on it as if to cool it off. He typed the name of the website into a search site. He leaned in to consult the screen. "Dang. The listing is private."

"Shoot," I muttered. But then my eye spotted something on the monitor still rolling the security camera footage. A small car drove by—a car painted in a shade of yellow-gold somewhere between the color of a school bus and processed cheese. I gasped. I recognized that car. I didn't know who it belonged to, but I'd seen it at the veterinarian's office. It was an unusual color. It couldn't be coincidence, could it? The likelihood seemed low that such a distinctive car would be at the vet's office and again here where Silly had been turned over unless it was the same car. *Had another of Dr. Burgess's clients have stolen Silly?*

Layla and I scurried back to her condo. As we burst through the door, I cried, "We have a lead!" I told Eleanor about the car I'd seen on the video. "The police can get the names of Dr. Burgess's other clients and find out which of them drives a gold Mitsubishi."

Unfortunately, we'd have to wait until the morning. The veterinary office was already closed for the day, and we had a four-hour drive back home ahead of us. But, first thing tomorrow morning, we'd be at the doctor's door.

Chapter Six

Officer Lorenzo had given me his business card, and Eleanor phoned him on our drive back to Atlanta. She explained the situation, and he agreed to meet us at the vet's office at eight o'clock the following morning.

Eleanor glanced back for the hundredth time at Silly, who was napping in her carrier in the back seat, then cast a grateful smile my way. "I appreciate everything you've done to help me get Silly back." Her eyes filled with tears and she choked up. "You're a peach."

"I'm happy I could help." My mind went to the other missing pets—Pierre, Chucky, and Itsy-Bitsy. Had the same person stolen and sold the dogs, too? I hoped that Officer Lorenzo could find out.

When we arrived back in Savannah, I scurried up to my apartment to retrieve Sherlock so he could welcome his bestie back home. The two cats were thrilled to see each other, chasing each other around one minute, then tangling on the rug and exchanging sloppy kisses the next.

Eleanor laughed. "I think Sherlock's nearly as happy to see Silly as I am!"

Given the late hour, my cat and I didn't stay long. The next morning, Eleanor was already waiting for me on her porch when I went to get her at a quarter to eight. She had a determined glint in her eye that matched the glint of the morning sun off her aluminum cane. She brandished the device. "Let's go bust some kneecaps!"

We climbed into my car and drove to the vet's office. As we pulled into the parking lot, I found myself agape. Officer Lorenzo's cruiser had yet to arrive, but the yellow-gold Mitsubishi sat at the end of the lot. Eleanor spotted it, too. "The pet thief is back!"

I snapped a quick photo of the car so that we'd have its license plate number in case the person left before Lorenzo arrived.

Eleanor opened her door.

"We should wait for the police," I said. "Let them handle it."

"You're right." Despite her words, she climbed out of the car. "But this won't be the first time I didn't do what I should."

Clearly, there was no stopping her. I couldn't blame her. If someone had stolen my sweet, smart Sherlock, I'd be eager to nail them, too. I climbed out and followed her into the office. She moved with such amazing speed, I half expected to see flames shooting out of the bottom of her cane.

Eleanor threw the door open and barreled into the lobby. I followed her inside. As usual, it smelled faintly of disinfectant. The faint sound of barking came from behind a closed door somewhere down the hall. My neighbor glanced around. Several patients waited in the reception area with their owners. A golden retriever with a bald man at the end of his leash. A scraggly terrier mix laying at the foot of a strawberry blonde. Two women with brown hair, one of whom cradled a calico cat in her arms and the other of whom held a quivering chihuahua on her lap. Both of the women wore glasses, but one sported cheap readers and the other wore wire frames. Neither wore the round, plastic style I'd seen on the person who'd impersonated Bonnie.

Eleanor demanded, "Who owns the yellow Mitsubishi?"

The clients shook their heads, but movement in the corner of my eye caught my attention. Felicity, the brown-haired, round-eyeglass-wearing receptionist rose slowly and silently from her seat behind the counter.

Eleanor must have spotted her, too. She turned and pointed her cane at the woman, her rage helping to keep her on her feet. "It was you," she hissed, like an angry cat. "Wasn't it?"

A tech standing at the counter frowned in confusion as her coworker grabbed her purse and circled around the desk, preparing to flee. But if Felicity thought she could make a quick and easy getaway, she was mistaken. As she attempted to run past Eleanor, my neighbor swung her cane and tripped the woman. Looked like Eleanor hadn't been joking about breaking kneecaps. Felicity fell forward, sprawling onto the floor, the contents of her purse scattering across the tile floor. While his owner watched, bewildered, the golden retriever snatched up her leather wallet and flopped down to chew on it.

While the pet thief was still prone, Eleanor raised her cane high over her head and brought it down on the woman's backside. *Whack!* Felicity cried out, but Eleanor showed her as much mercy as she deserved—none. *Whack!* I debated whether I should stop my neighbor, but I decided she deserved to meter out a bit of her own justice.

Officer Lorenzo came running through the door. He grabbed Eleanor's cane as she raised it again, and I, in turn, grabbed Eleanor to keep her from falling over. She pointed down. "It's her! She's the pet thief!"

The woman didn't even bother to deny it, she just burst into tears. But if she expected anyone to feel sorry for her, she would be severely disappointed. Her coworkers gathered in the lobby, casting her looks of utter disgust. In minutes, the officer had her in handcuffs, and was interrogating her in one of the examination rooms. He allowed me and Eleanor to sit in, along with the veterinarian.

Felicity averted her eyes as she spilled her guts. She admitted that she'd cased Eleanor's house, and borrowed a friend's white SUV to impersonate Bonnie. "I bought a cheap wig online and printed out the logo from the health agency from their website. I enlarged it on my computer and taped it to the door. I figured from far away nobody would be able to tell. I took some of Mrs. Potter's jewelry so it would look like a burglary."

So, I'd been right. The jewelry theft was a ruse. I felt a sense of smug satisfaction. Maybe if historic preservation didn't pan out, I could get a job as a detective or private investigator.

Felicity cut a look to Eleanor. "I still have the jewelry. I'll return it."

It was the right thing to do, but it wasn't going to get her off the hook.

Eleanor asked, "How did you catch Silly? She hates to be put in her carrier."

"Catnip," Felicity said. "I noticed you'd used it to get it into her carrier the day of her appointment, so I put a bunch of it in a bag I'd brought. She stepped right in and I zipped her up inside it."

That explained why the bag had seemed to be moving in her hands when I'd seen her out the window.

Lorenzo asked about the other missing purebred pets. "Did you steal them, too?"

She nodded. "People pay lots of money for pure breeds. My boyfriend moved out and stuck me with the lease. I was in a bind. I don't make enough to pay the rent by myself. Selling pets seemed like an easy way to make money."

Eleanor fumed next to me. I didn't blame her one bit. Felicity's easy money had caused untold amounts of grief to loving pet owners.

Dr. Burgess was mortified to learn that one of his staff had been involved in a pet theft ring. He was additionally mortified to learn that she'd stolen medication—the gabapentin—that was intended for his patients, and administered it to an elderly woman with health problems. He clenched his fists at his sides. "You could have killed her!"

"But I didn't." Felicity gestured to Eleanor and scoffed. "She's still here. I looked it up. I gave her the same dose as a Great Dane." Her initial remorse was clearly giving way to defensiveness, but there was no way she could ever justify what she had done, the risks she had taken with Eleanor's life, the pain she had caused both the owners and their pets.

I told both Officer Lorenzo and the veterinarian how I had tracked Silly down through her microchip registration. "Maybe the other missing pets can be located through the registry, too."

"We'll get right on that." Dr. Burgess left the room to assign the task to one of his staff. His practice would certainly lose some goodwill over this debacle, but if he could help reunite the missing pets with their owners, maybe he could salvage some of his reputation.

Officer Lorenzo hauled Felicity out to his cruiser. Eleanor whooped as he loaded the woman into his back seat. "I hope the judge throws the book at you!"

Her wish was mine, as well.

* * *

Eleanor, the other pet owners, and I crowded the benches in the courtroom the day of Felicity's sentencing. Eleanor had brought Silly with her. Many of the other pet owners had brought their pets, too. Pierre, the French bulldog, was in attendance, as were Chucky and Itsy-Bitsy.

Felicity had confessed to setting up the bogus pet rescue website and pocketing thousands of dollars in so-called adoption fees. She'd also confessed to drugging Eleanor. The district attorney had charged her with fraud, theft, assault, drug violations, and animal cruelty for causing the pets to suffer upon the separation from their owners and packs. Fortunately, most of the pets had been reunited with their owners, though some of the victims were still in negotiations or legal proceedings with the people who'd paid Felicity for the stolen pets.

With the facts established and not in dispute, the prosecutor had offered Felicity a plea deal under which she'd serve a two-year sentence and perform a thousand hours of community service. She'd refused the offer, against her own attorney's advice. In fact, she'd proceeded to fire her attorney, evidently thinking she could do a better job of defending herself.

After reading the file and listening to the D.A.'s summary, the seasoned, silver-haired judge looked down from her bench at Felicity. "Are you still refusing to accept the offer?"

"Absolutely." Felicity huffed. "It would be ridiculous for me to spend time in jail. Nobody was harmed. The pets weren't either. They've either been returned to their previous owners or remain in good homes. Some of the people have replaced their pets with new ones. What's the big deal?"

Pierre issued a sharp *arf* in indignation and the gallery murmured in agreement.

The judge glared down at the pet thief, shaking her head. "You also administered an unprescribed drug to a woman who'd suffered a stroke. That's a big deal, too."

Felicity flung a dismissive hand. "Gabapentin is a mild sedative. The woman survived." She hiked a thumb to indicate Eleanor. "She's right there. See? She suffered no long-term effects."

Fury boiled up inside me as I recalled how terrified I'd been to find Eleanor non-responsive, how traumatized she'd been to learn that she'd been drugged, her home had been burglarized, and, worst of all, her beloved cat had gone missing. It was all I could do to stay in my seat when every cell of my being wanted to hurdle the half wall separating me from the defendant and rip her to shreds.

Downplaying her actions was earning her no points with the court, either. The judge heaved a heavy sigh, reached into her robe, and pulled out a large locket on a chain. She opened the shiny heart and held it up to reveal the photos inside. Though we couldn't see the details from the gallery, we could see enough to tell that the photo of a black and white animal appeared on one side, and an orange one on the other. She pointed first to the left side, then the right. "This is my Dalmatian mix, Salvador, and this is my orange tabby, Tangerine. They bring me joy and mean the world to me. I mean the world to them, too. They count on me. Their lives depend on me. We need each other." She snapped the locket shut and pointed at the gallery, moving her finger to indicate all of us. "These victims loved their pets just as much as I love mine. For you to walk into my court and try to minimize the despicable things you've done and the incredible hurt you've caused is unconscionable. I hereby sentence you to seven years."

With that she brought down her gavel. *Bam!* We'd gotten our wish. *Hooray!* Felicity sputtered in rage and disbelief as she was hauled away.

Eleanor invited the other victims and their pets to her house to celebrate the victory in court. The local press came, too, and Eleanor provided an interview in which she warned anyone who owned pets, especially purebreds, to take extra precautions to ensure their safety. "Some people only see pets as property," she warned. "But the rest of us know better. They aren't property. They're family."

Silly looked up at Eleanor and purred loudly into the reporter's microphone, eliciting happy laughter from the crowd.

Eleanor reached out, grabbed me by the hand, and pulled me over to stand in front of the cameraman. "This is my neighbor and friend, Austen. She's the one who solved the case. We will all be forever grateful."

The others in attendance cheered, raised glasses of champagne, and called, "Hear, hear!"

I felt my cheeks heat with a blush, but I was proud to have helped reunite these pets with their owners.

When the party was over, I returned to my apartment to find Sherlock sitting in front of the window, watching the street, as usual. I scooped him up in my arms and scratched him under the chin. "I never could have solved the case without the help of my furry little detective."

The swish of his tail told me he fully agreed.

THE END

Note to Readers

Dear Reader,

I hope you enjoyed this story as much as I enjoyed writing it for you!

What did you think of this story? Posting reviews online are a great way to share your thoughts with fellow readers and help each other find stories best suited to your individual tastes.

Be the first to hear about upcoming releases, special discounts, and subscriber-only perks by signing up for my newsletter at my website, www.DianeKelly.com.

Find me on my Author Diane Kelly page on Facebook or at @DianeKellyBooks on Instagram.

I love to chat with book clubs! Contact me via my website if you'd like to arrange a virtual visit with your group.

See the following pages for a list of my other books, and visit my website for fun excerpts.

Happy reading! See you in the next story.

Diane

Other Books by Diane Kelly

MYSTERY NOVELLAS:
The Trouble With Digging Too Deep
Don't Toy With Me

THE BUSTED SERIES:
Busted
Another Big Bust
Busting Out

THE MOUNTAIN LODGE MYSTERIES:
Getaway with Murder
A Trip With Trouble
Snow Place for Murder

THE SOUTHERN HOMEBREW (MOONSHINE) SERIES:
The Moonshine Shack Murder
The Proof is in the Poison
Fiddling With Fate

THE HOUSE FLIPPER SERIES:
Dead as a Door Knocker
Dead in the Doorway
Murder With a View
Batten Down the Belfry
Primer and Punishment
Four-Alarm Homicide

Dead Post Society

The Barn Identity

THE PAW ENFORCEMENT SERIES:

Paw Enforcement

Paw and Order

Upholding the Paw (a bonus novella)

Laying Down the Paw

Against the Paw

Above the Paw

The Long Paw of the Law

Paw of the Jungle

Bending the Paw

Pawfully Wedded

THE TARA HOLLOWAY ("DEATH AND TAXES") SERIES:

Death, Taxes, and a French Manicure

Death, Taxes, and a Skinny No-Whip Latte

Death, Taxes, and Extra-Hold Hairspray

Death, Taxes, and a Sequined Clutch (a bonus novella)

Death, Taxes, and Peach Sangria

Death, Taxes, and Hot Pink Leg Warmers

Death, Taxes, and Green Tea Ice Cream

Death, Taxes, and Mistletoe Mayhem (a bonus novella)

Death, Taxes, and Silver Spurs

Death, Taxes, and Cheap Sunglasses

Death, Taxes, and a Chocolate Cannoli

Death, Taxes, and a Satin Garter

Death, Taxes, and Sweet Potato Fries
Death, Taxes, and Pecan Pie (a bonus novella)
Death, Taxes, and a Shotgun Wedding

ROMANCES:

Love Unleashed
Love, Luck, & Little Green Men
One Magical Night
A Sappy Love Story

Printed in Dunstable, United Kingdom